KNOCK KNOCK

JOKES

FOR

FUNNY KIDS

BY JIMMY JONES

Over 370 really FUNNY, HiLArious, LAUGH OUT LOUd KNOCK KNOCK JOKES FOr FUNNY KidS!

Jimmy Jones

<u>Books by Jimmy Jones</u>
Funny Jokes For Funny Kids
Knock Knock Jokes For Funny Kids

Funny Jokes For Kids Series
All Ages 5 -12!

To see all the latest books by
Jimmy Jones just go to
kidsjokebooks.com

CONTENTS

Jimmy Jones

Funny Knock Knock Jokes!

Knock knock.
Who's there?
Dishes.
Dishes who?
Dishes the police! Open up!

Knock knock.
Who's there?
Alpaca.
Alpaca who?
Alpaca the suitcase, you pack a the trunk!

Knock knock.
Who's there?
Athena.
Athena who?
Athena shooting star last night so I made a wish!

Knock knock.
Who's there?
Ida.
Ida who?
Ida like to speak with you about our new range of doorbells!

Knock knock knock.
Who's there?
Flea.
Flea who?
I knocked Flea times! Why didn't you answer?

Knock knock.
Who's there?
Honey bee.
Honey bee who?
Honey bee kind and open the door for your grandma!

Knock knock.
Who's there?
Henrietta.
Henrietta who?
Henrietta apple and he found half a worm!

Jimmy Jones

Knock knock.
Who's there?
Wooden Shoe.
Wooden shoe who?
Wooden shoe know it! Grandma finally got her driving licence!

Knock knock.
Who's there?
Leaf.
Leaf who?
Leaf the key under the mat next time!

Knock knock.
Who's there?
Dozen.
Dozen who?
Dozen anybody want to let me in? It's cold out here!

Knock knock.
Who's there?
Emma.
Emma who?
Emma very hungry! What's for lunch?

Knock Knock Jokes For Funny Kids

Knock knock.
Who's there?
Cheese.
Cheese who?
For cheese a jolly good fellow, for cheese a jolly good fellow!!

Knock knock.
Who's there?
Althea.
Althea who?
Althea later on, dude!

Knock knock.
Who's there?
Doris.
Doris who?
Doris a bit squeaky! I think you need to oil it!

Knock knock.
Who's there?
Pasta.
Pasta who?
Pasta salt and pepper please!

Jimmy Jones

Knock knock.
Who's there?
Phone.
Phone who?
Phonely I had known you were home I would have knocked earlier!

Knock knock.
Who's there?
Iran.
Iran who?
Iran really fast to get here and you're not even ready!

Knock knock.
Who's there?
Baby owl.
Baby owl who?
Baby owl see you at school next week!

Knock knock.
Who's there?
Aida.
Aida who?
Aida hamburger for lunch and now I'm full!

Knock Knock Jokes For Funny Kids

Knock knock.
Who's there?
Iva.
Iva who?
Iva very sore hand from all this knocking!

Knock knock.
Who's there?
Watson.
Watson who?
Watson the tv tonight? I feel like watching cartoons!

Knock knock.
Who's there?
Razor.
Razor who?
Razor hands in the air like you just don't care!

Knock knock.
Who's there?
Roach.
Roach who?
Roach you 3 letters but you never replied!

Jimmy Jones

Knock knock.
Who's there?
Gopher.
Gopher who?
I could Gopher a milkshake right now!

Knock knock.
Who's there?
Diet.
Diet who?
You can change your hair color if you diet!

Knock knock.
Who's there?
Mustache.
Mustache who?
I mustache you a question. Where were you on the night of the 15th?

Knock knock.
Who's there?
CD.
CD who?
CD car out the front? That's my new car! Woo Hoo!

Knock Knock Jokes For Funny Kids

Knock knock.
Who's there?
Harry.
Harry who?
Harry up it's so cold a penguin would freeze!

Knock knock.
Who's there?
Noah.
Noah who?
Noah good place for lunch? How about pizza?

Knock knock.
Who's there?
Garden.
Garden who?
Garden the treasure chest from the pirates. Aarrrrrr!

Knock knock.
Who's there?
Jimmy.
Jimmy who?
Jimmy 2 seconds and I will tell you all about it!

Jimmy Jones

Knock knock.
Who's there?
Al.
Al who?
Al tell you if you open this door and let me in!

Knock knock.
Who's there?
Ariel.
Ariel who?
Ariel lly want to come inside so let me in already!

Knock knock.
Who's there?
Jess.
Jess who?
Jess let me in please! It's cold out here!

Knock knock.
Who's there?
Peas.
Peas who?
Peas let me in! I really need to use the bathroom! It's an emergency!

Knock Knock Jokes For Funny Kids

Knock knock.
Who's there?
Cash.
Cash who?
You sound like you are a little bit nutty!

Knock knock.
Who's there?
Monacles.
Monacles who?
Monacles are sore from so much knocking. I think I need a band aid!

Knock knock.
Who's there?
Shemp.
Shemp who?
Shempoo your hair please, it looks dirty!

Knock knock.
Who's there?
Eddy.
Eddy who?
Eddy body home, I ran out of food!

Jimmy Jones

Knock knock.
Who's there?
Amos.
Amos who?
Amos say you look great in that suit. Where did you get it?

Knock knock.
Who's there?
Who Who.
Who Who Who?
How long have you had a pet owl?

Knock knock.
Who's there?
Duncan.
Duncan who?
Duncan doughnuts go really well with ice cream!

Knock knock.
Who's there?
Omar.
Omar who?
Omar goodness, that food smells delicious!

Knock Knock Jokes For Funny Kids

Knock knock.
Who's there?
Donna.
Donna who?
Donna want to make a big deal about it but your doorbell is broken!

Knock knock.
Who's there?
Icy.
Icy who?
Icy you through the keyhole! Please open up!

Knock knock.
Who's there?
Avery.
Avery who?
Avery big storm is coming! Please let me in!

Knock knock.
Who's there?
Orange.
Orange who?
Orange you glad I finally made it? Sorry I'm late!

Jimmy Jones

Knock knock.
Who's there?
Art.
Art who?
r2 d2!

Knock knock.
Who's there?
Lee.
Lee who?
Lee a key out for me next time and I won't have to knock!

Knock knock.
Who's there?
Hand.
Hand who?
Handover your money, this is a stick up!

Knock knock.
Who's there?
Ben.
Ben who?
Ben away for years but now I'm back! Let's party!!

Funnier Knock Knock Jokes!

Knock knock.
Who's there?
Kanye.
Kanye who?
Kanye give me a hand with this parcel? It's really heavy!

Knock knock.
Who's there?
Nanna.
Nanna who?
Nanna your business! It's top secret!

Knock knock.
Who's there?
Avenue.
Avenue who?
Avenue fixed the doorbell yet? It's still broken!

Knock knock.
Who's there?
Alison.
Alison who?
Alison to music all day long because I love it!

Knock knock.
Who's there?
Wire.
Wire who?
Wire you still inside? Let's go!

Knock knock.
Who's there?
Phillip.
Phillip who?
Phillip your pool so we can swim!

Knock knock.
Who's there?
Kim.
Kim who?
Kim here and give me a kiss. I have missed you so much!

Knock knock.
Who's there?
Fiddle.
Fiddle who?
Fiddle make you happy I'll keep telling jokes!

Knock knock.
Who's there?
Fangs.
Fangs who?
Fangs for letting me come to your party. It's gonna be fun!

Knock knock.
Who's there?
X.
X who?
X on toast for breakfast? Great idea!

Knock knock.
Who's there?
Hugo.
Hugo who?
Hugo where I go and I go where Hugo!

Knock knock.
Who's there?
Frank.
Frank who?
Frank ly speaking I would really like it if you fixed your doorbell!

Knock knock.
Who's there?
Turnip.
Turnip who?
Turnip the music! It's time to party!

Knock knock.
Who's there?
Sir.
Sir who?
Sir prise! I bet you weren't expecting me, were you?

Knock knock.
Who's there?
A pile up.
A pile up who?
Yeww! Stinky!

Knock Knock Jokes For Funny Kids

Knock knock.
Who's there?
Felix.
Felix who?
Felix my ice cream one more time he can buy me a new one!

Knock knock.
Who's there?
Tads.
Tads who?
It's Jimmy Jones, tads who!

Knock knock.
Who's there?
Ice cream soda.
Ice cream soda who?
Ice scream soda whole neighbourhood can hear me!

Knock knock.
Who's there?
Cheese.
Cheese who?
Cheese a very good singer. Want to see her new band?

Jimmy Jones

Knock knock.
Who's there?
Wanda.
Wanda who?
I Wanda come in and use your bathroom!

Knock knock.
Who's there?
Lionel.
Lionel who?
Lionel bite you if you put your arm in his mouth!

Knock knock.
Who's there?
Ice cream.
Ice cream who?
Ice cream when I jump in the pool! It's fun!

Knock knock.
Who's there?
Wooden.
Wooden who?
Wooden you like to let me in so I can give you your present?

Knock Knock Jokes For Funny Kids

Knock knock.
Who's there?
Boo.
Boo who?
Don't cry so much, it's not that sad!

Knock knock.
Who's there?
Yukon.
Yukon who?
Yukon say that again!

Knock knock.
Who's there?
Tyrone.
Tyrone who?
Tyrone shoe laces lazybones!

Knock knock.
Who's there?
Udder.
Udder who?
You look a bit Udder the weather! Are you sick?

Jimmy Jones

Knock knock.
Who's there?
Needle.
Needle who?
Needle hand to move your TV? I've got big muscles!

Knock knock.
Who's there?
Sancho.
Sancho who?
Sancho an email 2 days ago and you still haven't replied!

Knock knock.
Who's there?
Owl.
Owl who?
Owl be very happy when you finally open the door!

Knock knock.
Who's there?
West.
West who?
If you need a west from your homework, let's go!

Knock Knock Jokes For Funny Kids

Knock knock.
Who's there?
Hammond.
Hammond who?
Hammond eggs on toast! Yummy!

Knock knock.
Who's there?
Goose.
Goose who?
Goose who is here for dinner? Aunt Betty!

Knock knock.
Who's there?
Snow.
Snow who?
Snow use asking me! I'm 100 years old and can't remember a thing!

Knock knock.
Who's there?
Sofa.
Sofa who?
Sofa these jokes have been funny. Here's another one!

Jimmy Jones

Knock knock.
Who's there?
Cook.
Cook who?
Are you a cuckoo clock?

Knock knock.
Who's there?
Hijack.
Hijack who?
HiJack! Is Jill Home?

Knock knock.
Who's there?
Ben.
Ben who?
Ben knocking so long my hand feels like it's going to fall off!

Knock knock.
Who's there?
Comb.
Comb who?
Comb outside and I will tell you!

Knock Knock Jokes For Funny Kids

Knock knock.
Who's there?
Olive.
Olive who?
Olive here but I forgot my key!

Knock knock.
Who's there?
Ivor.
Ivor who?
Ivor you open the door or I will climb through the window!

Knock knock.
Who's there?
Soomie.
Soomie who?
If you Soomie I will sue you!

Knock knock.
Who's there?
Dumbbell.
Dumbbell who?
Dumbbell needs to be fixed so I don't have to knock!

28

Jimmy Jones

Knock knock.
Who's there?
Yoda Lady.
Yoda Lady who?
You are such a great yodeller!

Knock knock.
Who's there?
Mabel.
Mabel who?
Mabel works but yours is broken. Ha Ha!!

Knock knock.
Who's there?
Dewey.
Dewey who?
Dewey have to go to school tomorrow? My favorite band is in town!

Knock knock.
Who's there?
Yorkies.
Yorkies who?
Yorkies are needed to open this door!

Knock knock.
Who's there?
Isabel.
Isabel who?
I know there Isabel but I like knocking!

Knock knock.
Who's there?
Value.
Value who?
Value open the door before this ice cream melts?

Knock knock.
Who's there?
Sam.
Sam who?
Sam day I will remember my key and then I won't have to knock!

Knock knock.
Who's there?
A little old lady.
A little old lady who?
I didn't know you went to yodelling school!

Crazy Knock Knock Jokes!

Knock knock.
Who's there?
Kenya.
Kenya who?
Kenya please hurry up and open this door! It's really cold out here!

Knock knock.
Who's there?
York.
York who?
York ar seems to have a flat tire!

Knock knock.
Who's there?
Quacker.
Quacker who?
Quacker another funny joke and I might pee my pants!

Knock Knock Jokes For Funny Kids

Knock knock.
Who's there?
Fanny.
Fanny who?
Fanny body knocks just pretend you're not home!

Knock knock.
Who's there?
Wanda.
Wanda who?
I Wanda what we can do with all this money my aunt gave me?

Knock knock.
Who's there?
Canoe.
Canoe who?
Canoe help me fix my flat tire?

Knock knock.
Who's there?
Tweet.
Tweet who?
Would you like tweet an apple? They are really tasty!

Jimmy Jones

Knock knock.
Who's there?
Oliver.
Oliver who?
Oliver other kids are busy so can you help me do my chores?

Knock knock.
Who's there?
Rhino.
Rhino who?
Rhino all the funniest knock knock jokes!

Knock knock.
Who's there?
Voodoo.
Voodoo who?
Voodoo you think you are, making me wait so long!

Knock knock.
Who's there?
Iva.
Iva who?
Iva feeling we have met before somewhere!

Knock knock.
Who's there?
Kent.
Kent who?
Kent you see I want to come in already! I've been waiting for 3 hours!

Knock knock.
Who's there?
Thermos.
Thermos who?
Thermos be a quicker way to open this door!

Knock knock.
Who's there?
Boo.
Boo who?
It's not that sad! Pull yourself together!

Knock knock.
Who's there?
Barbara.
Barbara who?
Barbara black sheep, have you any wool?

Jimmy Jones

Knock knock.
Who's there?
Gerald.
Gerald who?
It's Gerald friend from school! Don't you recognize me?

Knock knock.
Who's there?
Phil.
Phil who?
Phil the car please, we're low on gas!

Knock knock.
Who's there?
Radio.
Radio who?
Radio not, I'm coming in!

Knock knock.
Who's there?
Bat.
Bat who?
Bat you will never guess who it is!

Knock Knock Jokes For Funny Kids

Knock knock.
Who's there?
Jamaica.
Jamaica who?
Jamaica mistake? You forgot to leave the key under the mat!

Knock knock.
Who's there?
Freddy.
Freddy who?
Freddy or not, here I come!

Knock knock.
Who's there?
Omar.
Omar who?
Omar goodness I love your shirt! Where did you get it?

Knock knock.
Who's there?
Dozen.
Dozen who?
Dozen all this knocking get a bit annoying? Ha Ha!!

Jimmy Jones

Knock knock.
Who's there?
Leah.
Leah who?
Leah the door unlocked next time, and then I won't have to knock!

Knock knock.
Who's there?
Lego.
Lego who?
Lego of the handle so I can open this door!

Knock knock.
Who's there?
Terrain.
Terrain who?
It's starting terrain, do you have an umbrella?

Knock knock.
Who's there?
Voodoo.
Voodoo who?
Voodoo you think it is knocking? Santa Claus?

Knock knock.
Who's there?
Claire.
Claire who?
Claire the way! Skateboarder coming through!

Knock knock.
Who's there?
Iona.
Iona who?
Iona brand new car! Come and see!

Knock knock.
Who's there?
Ancient.
Ancient who?
Ancient going to let me in. I'm late for dinner!

Knock knock.
Who's there?
Candice.
Candice who?
Candice door open any quicker please?

Jimmy Jones

Knock knock.
Who's there?
Tank.
Tank who?
You're very welcome madam!

Knock knock.
Who's there?
Cash.
Cash who?
Actually I prefer peanuts mixed with almonds!

Knock knock.
Who's there?
Bass.
Bass who?
Bass ball is fun so let's go and play!

Knock knock.
Who's there?
Robin.
Robin who?
He's Robin your house! Call the Police!

Knock knock.
Who's there?
Waiter.
Waiter who?
Waiter I tell your mom! You're in trouble now!

Knock knock.
Who's there?
Isabel.
Isabel who?
Isabel working yet so I can stop knocking?

Knock knock.
Who's there?
Avenue.
Avenue who?
Avenue seen the news! Quick! Let's go!

Knock knock.
Who's there?
Meg.
Meg who?
Meg up your mind and let me in!

Jimmy Jones

Knock knock.
Who's there?
Major.
Major who?
Major day with all these jokes, didn't I?

Knock knock.
Who's there?
Sarah.
Sarah who?
Sarah problem with your door because I can't open it!

Knock knock.
Who's there?
Ash.
Ash who?
Bless you! Would you like a tissue?

Knock knock.
Who's there?
Howl.
Howl who?
Howl you know if you don't ever open up this door!

Knock Knock Jokes For Funny Kids

Knock knock.
Who's there?
Will.
Will who?
Will you let me in before I freeze?

Knock knock.
Who's there?
Tennis.
Tennis who?
Tennis five plus five! I'm good at math!!

Knock knock.
Who's there?
Don.
Don who?
Don t ya want to open the door before I freeze to death!

Knock knock.
Who's there?
Max.
Max who?
Max no difference to me as I can't remember my last name!

Jimmy Jones

Knock knock.
Who's there?
Stopwatch.
Stopwatch who?
Stopwatch you're doing and let me in!

Knock knock.
Who's there?
Fanny.
Fanny who?
Fanny body home? Why don't you answer?

Knock knock.
Who's there?
Gladys.
Gladys who?
Gladys Friday – I love the weekend! Yayy!

Knock knock.
Who's there?
Dishes.
Dishes who?
Dishes me, remember? We met last week!

Silly Knock Knock Jokes!

Knock knock.
Who's there?
House.
House who?
House about letting me in before I fall asleep!

Knock knock.
Who's there?
Robin.
Robin who?
Robin you! Hands up and fill my bag with money!

Knock knock.
Who's there?
Alby.
Alby who?
Alby back in a minute, so just wait there please!

Jimmy Jones

Knock knock.
Who's there?
Irish.
Irish who?
Irish I was taller. Then I could reach the doorbell!

Knock knock.
Who's there?
Ice cream.
Ice cream who?
Ice Cream if you don't open this door right now!

Knock knock.
Who's there?
Weirdo.
Weirdo who?
Weirdo you want me to put your parcel, sir? Please sign here.

Knock knock.
Who's there?
Amish.
Amish who?
You're not a shoe, you're a person!

Knock Knock Jokes For Funny Kids

Knock knock.
Who's there?
King Tut.
King Tut who?
King Tut key fried chicken for dinner tonight!

Knock knock.
Who's there?
Smell Mype.
Smell Mype who?
No thanks! Too smelly!

Knock knock.
Who's there?
Carmen.
Carmen who?
Carmen get your hotdogs! Fresh hotdogs for sale!

Knock knock.
Who's there?
Justin.
Justin who?
Justin case I forget my key can you leave it out for me?

Jimmy Jones

Knock knock.
Who's there?
Owl.
Owl who?
Owl be sure to use the doorbell tomorrow!

Knock knock.
Who's there?
Herd.
Herd who?
I herd you were home. Why didn't you call?

Knock knock.
Who's there?
Claire.
Claire who?
Claire the way! I need to use the bathroom! Quickly!

Knock knock.
Who's there?
Needle.
Needle who?
Needle little help with the shopping! I bought too much!

Knock Knock Jokes For Funny Kids

Knock knock.
Who's there?
Tish.
Tish who?
No thanks I use a handkerchief!

Knock knock.
Who's there?
Noise.
Noise who?
Noise to see you again after all this time!

Knock knock.
Who's there?
Ozzie.
Ozzie who?
Ozzie you later on, dude!

Knock knock.
Who's there?
Annie.
Annie who?
Annie idea when this rain will stop? I'm getting wet!

Jimmy Jones

Knock knock.
Who's there?
A Tish.
A Tish who?
I think you need to see a doctor!

Knock knock.
Who's there?
Ida.
Ida who?
Ida rather be inside than out here in the rain!

Knock knock.
Who's there?
Candice.
Candice who?
Candice door open any faster if I push it?

Knock knock.
Who's there?
Four eggs.
Four eggs who?
Four eggs-ample why don't you get a doorbell?

Knock Knock Jokes For Funny Kids

Knock knock.
Who's there?
Butter.
Butter who?
I Butter hurry up and come inside!

Knock knock.
Who's there?
Alfie.
Alfie who?
Alfie terrible if you don't invite me to your party!

Knock knock.
Who's there?
Arfur.
Arfur who?
Arfur got why I came over!

Knock knock.
Who's there?
Cupid.
Cupid who?
Cupid quiet! I'm trying to sleep here!

Jimmy Jones

Knock knock.
Who's there?
Venice.
Venice who?
Venice your dad getting home? He's late!

Knock knock.
Who's there?
Andy.
Andy who?
Andy runs so fast and he always wins!

Knock knock.
Who's there?
Eggs.
Eggs who?
Its eggstremely hot out here so please let me in!

Knock knock.
Who's there?
Kenya.
Kenya who?
Kenya guess who is coming to my place for dinner?

Knock knock.
Who's there?
Abbott.
Abbott who?
Abbott you I can climb that tree in less than a minute!

Knock knock.
Who's there?
Wood Ant.
Wood Ant who?
I Wood Ant want to be you when your mom gets home!

Knock knock.
Who's there?
Sherwood.
Sherwood who?
Sherwood would like to come in before it gets dark!

Knock knock.
Who's there?
Spell.
Spell who?
OK   W. H. O.

Jimmy Jones

Knock knock.
Who's there?
Godiva.
Godiva who?
Godiva bad headache. I need to lie down!

Knock knock.
Who's there?
Butter.
Butter who?
I butter tell you some more jokes before you get bored!

Knock knock.
Who's there?
Water.
Water who?
Water you doing later on today? Let's play some Xbox!

Knock knock.
Who's there?
Yeast.
Yeast who?
The yeast you can do is let me in! I've been waiting for ages!

Knock knock.
Who's there?
Heaven.
Heaven who?
Heaven seen you in ages! You're looking good!

Knock knock.
Who's there?
Lettuce.
Lettuce who?
Lettuce in please. We are really tired!

Knock knock.
Who's there?
Says.
Says who?
Says me, that's who! Ha Ha!

Knock knock.
Who's there?
Abby.
Abby who?
Abby stung me on my foot. OWWWWWWWW!!

Jimmy Jones

Knock knock.
Who's there?
Hannah.
Hannah who?
Hanna partridge in a pear tree!

Knock knock.
Who's there?
Alden.
Alden who?
When you're Alden with your homework, let's go fishing!

Knock knock.
Who's there?
Olive.
Olive who?
Olive you lots and lots you know!

Knock knock.
Who's there?
Canoe.
Canoe who?
Canoe come outside to play?

Knock Knock Jokes For Funny Kids

Knock knock.
Who's there?
Hank.
Hank who?
You are so welcome madam!

Knock knock.
Who's there?
Cereal.
Cereal who?
Cereal pleasure to meet you today my good sir!

Knock knock.
Who's there?
Barbie.
Barbie who?
Barbie Q Chicken for dinner? Yummmmm!!

Knock knock.
Who's there?
Frank.
Frank who?
Frank you very much for finally opening this door.

Jimmy Jones

Laugh Out Loud Knock Knock Jokes!

Knock knock.
Who's there?
Chicken.
Chicken who?
Let's chicken to that new hotel in town!

Knock knock.
Who's there?
Icing.
Icing who?
Icing so loud I need earplugs!

Knock knock.
Who's there?
Quiet Tina.
Quiet Tina who?
Quiet Tina Library! I'm trying to read!

Knock knock.
Who's there?
Owls say.
Owls say who?
Yes they do! You are now an Owl expert!

Knock knock.
Who's there?
Ferdie.
Ferdie who?
Ferdie last time please open up!

Knock knock.
Who's there?
Waa.
Waa who?
You sure are excited considering all I did was knock!

Knock knock.
Who's there?
Pecan.
Pecan who?
Pecan someone your own size you bully!

Jimmy Jones

Knock knock.
Who's there?
Yacht.
Yacht who?
Yacht to be able to recognize me. I only saw you last week!

Knock knock.
Who's there?
Gino.
Gino who?
Gino me really well so open the door!

Knock knock.
Who's there?
Pasta.
Pasta who?
It's Pasta your bedtime! Quick! Into bed!

Knock knock.
Who's there?
Wok.
Wok who?
Wok and woll baby!

Knock knock.
Who's there?
Gwen.
Gwen who?
Gwen you have finished your homework, let's go fishing!

Knock knock.
Who's there?
Kanye.
Kanye who?
Kanye please open this door before it starts to rain!

Knock knock.
Who's there?
Mikey.
Mikey who?
Mikey is too big for the keyhole! Noooooo!

Knock knock.
Who's there?
Lettuce.
Lettuce who?
Please lettuce in before our ice cream melts!

Jimmy Jones

Knock knock.
Who's there?
Detail.
Detail who?
Detail of your cat is so fluffy I want to tickle your chin with it!

Knock knock.
Who's there?
Keanu.
Keanu who?
Keanu open this door before I freeze to death!

Knock knock.
Who's there?
Honeydew.
Honeydew who?
Honeydew you want to hear lots more jokes?

Knock knock.
Who's there?
Poll.
Poll who?
Poll iceman John here. You're under arrest!

Knock Knock Jokes For Funny Kids

Knock knock.
Who's there?
Area.
Area who?
Area deaf! I've been knocking for 2 days!

Knock knock.
Who's there?
Annette.
Annette who?
The best way to catch a butterfly is with Annette! Let's try to catch one!

Knock knock.
Who's there?
Toby.
Toby who?
Toby or not to be, that is the question!

Knock knock.
Who's there?
Maul.
Maul who?
Let's go to the Maul and buy some treats!

Jimmy Jones

Knock knock.
Who's there?
Betty.
Betty who?
Betty you can't guess how many times I have knocked on this door!

Knock knock.
Who's there?
Norway.
Norway who?
That's Norway to talk to a friend!

Knock knock.
Who's there?
Ben.
Ben who?
Ben knocking so long I forgot why I'm here!

Knock knock.
Who's there?
Egg.
Egg who?
It's so Eggciting to see you again!

Knock knock.
Who's there?
Europe.
Europe who?
No I'm not! That's very rude!

Knock knock.
Who's there?
Mayan
Mayan who?
A Mayan the way? Should I move?

Knock knock.
Who's there?
Barbie.
Barbie who?
Barbie Q for dinner! Yummy!

Knock knock.
Who's there?
Boo.
Boo who?
Don't cry so much, it's only a joke!

Jimmy Jones

Knock knock.
Who's there?
Pop.
Pop who?
Pop on over to my place we're having ice cream!

Knock knock.
Who's there?
Tank.
Tank who?
Tank goodness you finally answered the door!

Knock knock.
Who's there?
Amanda.
Amanda who?
Amanda repair that window you broke wants to charge me $300!

Knock knock.
Who's there?
Howard.
Howard who?
Howard you like to knock for a change?

Knock Knock Jokes For Funny Kids

Knock knock.
Who's there?
Jupiter.
Jupiter who?
Jupiter invite in my letterbox? It looks like your writing.

Knock knock.
Who's there?
Tunis.
Tunis who?
Tunis company but three's a crowd!

Knock knock.
Who's there?
Alex.
Alex who?
Alex plain it all to you in a minute! Let me in!

Knock knock.
Who's there?
Norma Lee.
Norma Lee who?
Norma Lee I wouldn't knock but I forgot my key!

Jimmy Jones

Knock knock.
Who's there?
Howell.
Howell who?
Howell you find out if you never open this door!

Knock knock.
Who's there?
Athena.
Athena who?
Athena bear in your house so RUN!!!!!

Knock knock.
Who's there?
Nose.
Nose who?
I Nose plenty more Knock knock jokes for you!

Knock knock.
Who's there?
Hada.
Hada who?
Hada great weekend, how about you?

Knock Knock Jokes For Funny Kids

Knock knock.
Who's there?
Police.
Police who?
Police hurry up and open this door!

Knock knock.
Who's there?
Toucan.
Toucan who?
Toucan play that sort of game!

Knock knock.
Who's there?
Herbert.
Herbert who?
I like Herbert her friend is a bit annoying!

Knock knock.
Who's there?
Argo.
Argo who?
Argo to school in the morning, but first I need some sleep!

Jimmy Jones

Knock knock.
Who's there?
Eliza.
Eliza who?
Eliza quite a bit so I never believe him!

Knock knock.
Who's there?
Yvette.
Yvette who?
Yvette helps sick animals get better!

Knock knock.
Who's there?
Dish.
Dish who?
Dish is a very nice house you have here!

Knock knock.
Who's there?
Viper.
Viper who?
Viper nose before you get sick!

Ridiculous Knock Knock Jokes!

Knock knock.
Who's there?
Gorilla.
Gorilla who?
I can gorilla burger for you for your lunch if you like.

Knock knock.
Who's there?
Ada.
Ada who?
Ada sandwich for my lunch and it was yummy!

Knock knock.
Who's there?
Window.
Window who?
Window you have time to come over to my house?

Jimmy Jones

Knock knock.
Who's there?
Luke.
Luke who?
Luke through the window and find out!

Knock knock.
Who's there?
Annie.
Annie who?
Annie body home? I've bought you a present!

Knock knock.
Who's there?
Oscar.
Oscar who?
Oscar locksmith to open this door if you lost your key!

Knock knock.
Who's there?
Hamish.
Hamish who?
Hamish you so much when I don't see you.

Knock knock.
Who's there?
Amarillo.
Amarillo who?
Amarillo nice guy! Just ask me!

Knock knock.
Who's there?
Dragon.
Dragon who?
I'm dragon my feet because I have a sore leg!

Knock knock.
Who's there?
Locky.
Locky who?
Locky I caught you before you went out!

Knock knock.
Who's there?
Fork.
Fork who?
Fork got to mention, why is your doorbell broken?

Jimmy Jones

Knock knock.
Who's there?
Troy.
Troy who?
Troy to answer quicker next time please!

Knock knock.
Who's there?
Urine.
Urine who?
Urine allot of trouble if you don't open this door!

Knock knock.
Who's there?
Kanga.
Kanga who?
No, kangaroo!

Knock knock.
Who's there?
Aloha.
Aloha who?
Aloha bell would be handy because then I could reach it!

Knock Knock Jokes For Funny Kids

Knock knock.
Who's there?
Waiter.
Waiter who?
Waiter I finish telling all these jokes! Then I'll tell you some more!

Knock knock.
Who's there?
Daisy.
Daisy who?
Daisy me running but 'dey can't catch me!

Knock knock.
Who's there?
CD.
Cd who?
CD big clouds? It's gonna rain!

Knock knock.
Who's there?
Will.
Will who?
Will you marry me?

Jimmy Jones

Knock knock.
Who's there?
Wire.
Wire who?
Wire we talking through this door? Open up already!

Knock knock.
Who's there?
Bean.
Bean who?
Bean waiting here for ages! Why are you always late?

Knock knock.
Who's there?
Omelette.
Omelette who?
Omelette ing you come to my party if you open the door!

Knock knock.
Who's there?
Alpaca.
Alpaca who?
Alpaca my bags in the morning and be on my way!

Knock knock.
Who's there?
Teresa.
Teresa who?
Teresa very green this time of year!

Knock knock.
Who's there?
Todd.
Todd who?
Todd ay is the your lucky day because I'm here!

Knock knock.
Who's there?
Anne.
Anne who?
Anne imals are fun so let's go to the zoo and play with the tigers!

Knock knock.
Who's there?
Sadie.
Sadie who?
Sadie magic word and your wish will come true!

Jimmy Jones

Knock knock.
Who's there?
Howard.
Howard who?
Howard you like to go to the park and play ball?

Knock knock.
Who's there?
Riot.
Riot who?
I'm Riot on time so let's go!

Knock knock.
Who's there?
I am.
I am who?
Actually you are you!

Knock knock.
Who's there?
Grub.
Grub who?
Grub hold of my hand and I will show you the way!

Knock Knock Jokes For Funny Kids

Knock knock.
Who's there?
Figs.
Figs who?
Figs the bell please, this knocking is so last year!

Knock knock.
Who's there?
Doughnut.
Doughnut who?
I Doughnut know but I will find out!

Knock knock.
Who's there?
Candice.
Candice who?
Candice bell actually ring because I have pressed it 12 times already!

Knock knock.
Who's there?
Mary.
Mary who?
Mary Christmas to you and a happy new year!

Jimmy Jones

Knock knock.
Who's there?
Bed.
Bed who?
Bed you I can run faster than you. Ready, set, GO!!

Knock knock.
Who's there?
Irish.
Irish who?
Irish you knew some funny jokes too!

Knock knock.
Who's there?
Kermit.
Kermit who?
Kermit any crimes and the police will get you!

Knock knock.
Who's there?
UCI.
UCI who?
UCI am going to the park. Want to come?

Knock knock.
Who's there?
Toucan.
Toucan who?
Toucan play at this game you know!

Knock knock.
Who's there?
Ray.
Ray who?
Ray member when we first met? Love at first sight!

Knock knock.
Who's there?
Emerson.
Emerson who?
Emerson nice socks you have on. Did you get them at Kmart?

Knock knock.
Who's there?
Mushroom.
Mushroom who?
There wasn't mushroom at the party so I left!

Jimmy Jones

Knock knock.
Who's there?
Zany.
Zany who?
Zany body home today? Let me in!

Knock knock.
Who's there?
Loaf.
Loaf who?
I loaf pizza! Do you want some?

Knock knock.
Who's there?
Earl.
Earl who?
Earl be very happy when you let me in!

Knock knock.
Who's there?
Tooth.
Tooth who?
The Tooth, the whole tooth and nothing but the tooth!

Knock knock.
Who's there?
Sweden.
Sweden who?
Let's have Sweden Sour chicken for lunch! Yumm!

Knock knock.
Who's there?
Imma.
Imma who?
Imma getting a bit wet out here in the rain! Let me in!

Knock knock.
Who's there?
Mikey.
Mikey who?
Mikey doesn't fit! Why did you change the lock?

Knock knock.
Who's there?
Otto.
Otto who?
Otto know but I can't remember!

Jimmy Jones

Knock knock.
Who's there?
Leaf.
Leaf who?
If we Leaf now we can get there on time!

Knock knock.
Who's there?
Lock.
Lock who?
Lock who it is after all these years!

Knock knock.
Who's there?
Duncan.
Duncan who?
Duncan a cookie in milk is fun!

Knock knock.
Who's there?
Andrew.
Andrew who?
Andrew a very nice picture of you. Do you want to see?

Even Funnier Knock Knock Jokes!

Knock knock.
Who's there?
Wire.
Wire who?
Wire you taking so long to open the door?

Knock knock.
Who's there?
Dwayne.
Dwayne who?
Dwayne the pool quickly! I think Billy Bob fell in!

Knock knock.
Who's there?
Pudding.
Pudding who?
Pudding my new shoes on . Do you like them?

84

Jimmy Jones

Knock knock.
Who's there?
Nick.
Nick who?
You answered just in the nick of time, I need to pee!

Knock knock.
Who's there?
Ken.
Ken who?
Ken I please have a drink? I am so thirsty!

Knock knock.
Who's there?
Java.
Java who?
Java cup of sugar for my mom?

Knock knock.
Who's there?
Aisle.
Aisle who?
Aisle be over at Jack's place if you need me!

Knock knock.
Who's there?
Hawaii.
Hawaii who?
Great thanks, Hawaii you?

Knock knock.
Who's there?
Justin.
Justin who?
Justin case you didn't know, it's going to rain in a minute!

Knock knock.
Who's there?
Dora.
Dora who?
Dora's locked so should I climb through the window?

Knock knock.
Who's there?
Scold.
Scold who?
Scold enough today to make a snowman!

Jimmy Jones

Knock knock.
Who's there?
Jamaica.
Jamaica who?
Jamaica big mistake by answering the door! This is the Police! Hands up!

Knock knock.
Who's there?
Freeze.
Freeze who?
Freeze a jolly good fellowwww!

Knock knock.
Who's there?
Cannelloni.
Cannelloni who?
Cannelloni 5 bucks until next week?

Knock knock.
Who's there?
Leon.
Leon who?
You can Leon me if your leg is still sore!

Knock Knock Jokes For Funny Kids

Knock knock.
Who's there?
Abby.
Abby who?
Abby new year! Let's celebrate!

Knock knock.
Who's there?
Sacha.
Sacha who?
Sacha lot of questions for this time of day!

Knock knock.
Who's there?
Tahiti.
Tahiti who?
Tahiti home run you need to hit the ball really hard!

Knock knock.
Who's there?
Hannah.
Hannah who?
Hannah one and a two and a three and a four!

Jimmy Jones

Knock knock.
Who's there?
Beth.
Beth who?
Beth friends stick together so let's go!

Knock knock.
Who's there?
Armageddon.
Armageddon who?
Armageddon tired of knocking on this door!

Knock knock.
Who's there?
Les.
Les who?
Les go to the beach while it's still sunny!

Knock knock.
Who's there?
Bruce.
Bruce who?
I have a Bruce on my leg from when I fell over!

Knock knock.
Who's there?
Irish.
Irish who?
Irish you could come to my place for dinner. Mom's making pizza!

Knock knock.
Who's there?
Iowa.
Iowa who?
Iowa big apology to your mom. Is she in?

Knock knock.
Who's there?
Nun.
Nun who?
Nun of your business my good sir!

Knock knock.
Who's there?
Where what.
Where what who?
You forgot to ask why!

Jimmy Jones

Knock knock.
Who's there?
Howard.
Howard who?
Howard you like to have a turn at knocking as my hand is getting sore!

Knock knock.
Who's there?
Freddy.
Freddy who?
Freddy set, go! I'll race you to the letterbox!

Knock knock.
Who's there?
Icing.
Icing who?
Icing many songs. Which one would you like to hear?

Knock knock.
Who's there?
Lena.
Lena who?
Lena bit closer and I'll tell you all about it!

Knock knock.
Who's there?
Soda.
Soda who?
Soda you want to let me in or what?

Knock knock.
Who's there?
Utah.
Utah who?
Utah one who asked me over! Remember?

Knock knock.
Who's there?
Nobel.
Nobel who?
Nobel so I have to knock knock!

Knock knock.
Who's there?
Ben.
Ben who?
Ben meaning to call in for ages! How have you been?

Jimmy Jones

Knock knock.
Who's there?
Flicker.
Flicker who?
Flicker ice cream she won't be happy at all!

Knock knock.
Who's there?
Early Tibet.
Early Tibet who?
Early Tibet and early to rise!

Knock knock.
Who's there?
Adore.
Adore who?
Adore is between us. Open it now!

Knock knock.
Who's there?
Figs.
Figs who?
Please figs your step. I nearly tripped!

Knock knock.
Who's there?
Wayne.
Wayne who?
Wayne is due shortly so bring in your washing!

Knock knock.
Who's there?
Henrietta.
Henrietta who?
Henrietta too mucha spaghetti!

Knock knock.
Who's there?
Obi wan.
Obi wan who?
Obi Wan of your best friends! Let me in!

Knock knock.
Who's there?
Safari.
Safari who?
Safari so goody!

Jimmy Jones

Knock knock.
Who's there?
Figs.
Figs who?
Figs the doorbell please. All this knocking is so last year!

Knock knock.
Who's there?
Jester.
Jester who?
Jester minute! Where's your doorbell?

Knock knock.
Who's there?
Harry.
Harry who?
Harry up we have to go! Quick!

Knock knock.
Who's there?
Amma.
Amma who?
Amma not going to tell you until you open this door!

Bonus
Knock Knock Jokes!

Knock knock.
Who's there?
Howard.
Howard who?
Howard I know what Howard's last name is? I only just met him!

Knock knock.
Who's there?
Razor.
Razor who?
Razor hands, this is a stick up!

Knock knock.
Who's there?
House.
House who?
House it going my oldest friend?

Jimmy Jones

Knock knock.
Who's there?
Philip.
Philip who?
Philip up the pool so we can have a swim! It's so hot!

Knock knock.
Who's there?
Halibut.
Halibut who?
Halibut we go out to the mall and get a milkshake!

Knock knock.
Who's there?
Lion.
Lion who?
Lion down because I'm really tired! Goodnight!

Knock knock.
Who's there?
Water.
Water who?
Water beautiful day! I love the sun!

Knock Knock Jokes For Funny Kids

Knock knock.
Who's there?
Summer.
Summer who?
Summer my friends like funny jokes. How about you?

Knock knock.
Who's there?
Wanda.
Wanda who?
Wanda go and kick a soccer ball in the park?

Knock knock.
Who's there?
Luke.
Luke who?
Luke out the window and you will see for yourself!

Knock knock.
Who's there?
Amy.
Amy who?
Amy fraid I can't remember!

Jimmy Jones

Knock knock.
Who's there?
Noah.
Noah who?
Noah good place for a pizza? I'm really hungry!

Knock knock.
Who's there?
Amos.
Amos who?
Amos quito ZZZZZZZZZZZZ!!

Knock knock.
Who's there?
Jim.
Jim who?
Jim mind if I stay for a while? I got locked out of my own house!

Knock knock.
Who's there?
Red.
Red who?
Red quite a few jokes today so let's read a few more!

Knock Knock Jokes For Funny Kids

Knock knock.
Who's there?
Candy.
Candy who?
Candy door be answered faster next time please?

Knock knock.
Who's there?
Cray.
Cray who?
Cray-zee how long it took you to answer this door! I nearly gave up!

Knock knock.
Who's there?
Hippo.
Hippo who?
Hippo birthday to you! Hippo birthday to you!

Knock knock.
Who's there?
Doughnut.
Doughnut who?
I doughnut know, I forgot my name!

Jimmy Jones

Knock knock.
Who's there?
Dunnip.
Dunnip who?
I thought I could smell something! You might need to change your underwear!

Knock knock.
Who's there?
Jester.
Jester who?
Jester second! Why are you in my house?

Knock knock.
Who's there?
Chicken.
Chicken who?
Better chicken the oven! Something is burning!

Knock knock.
Who's there?
Cher.
Cher who?
Cher would like to come in before it gets dark!

Knock Knock Jokes For Funny Kids

Knock knock.
Who's there?
John.
John who?
If we John forces we could do anything!

Knock knock.
Who's there?
Stew.
Stew who?
Stew early to go home! Let's go to the park!

Knock knock.
Who's there?
Beef.
Beef who?
Beef-ore I freeze please open this door!

Knock knock.
Who's there?
Gopher.
Gopher who?
Gopher help quick! I think I broke my leg!
Owwww!!

Jimmy Jones

Knock knock.
Who's there?
Police.
Police who?
Police let me in! It's way too hot out here!

Knock knock.
Who's there?
Stork.
Stork who?
Better stork up on candles before the big storm!

Knock knock.
Who's there?
Pudding.
Pudding who?
Pudding on my walking shoes! Let's go for a hike!

Knock knock.
Who's there?
Van.
Van who?
Van are you going to let me in? I'm hungry!!

Knock knock.
Who's there?
Icy.
Icy who?
Icy you had a haircut. It looks great!

Knock knock.
Who's there?
Toad.
Toad who?
I toad you these jokes would be really funny!

Knock knock.
Who's there?
Bacon.
Bacon who?
I'm bacon a cake for your birthday! Do you want chocolate or fruit cake?

Knock knock.
Who's there?
Seymour.
Seymour who?
I Seymour when I wear my glasses!

Jimmy Jones

Knock knock.
Who's there?
Witches.
Witches who?
Witches the fastest way to my house from here?

Knock knock.
Who's there?
Lefty.
Lefty who?
Lefty key at home so I had to knock!

Knock knock.
Who's there?
Pasture.
Pasture who?
It's way pasture bedtime! Go to bed!

Knock knock.
Who's there?
Miles.
Miles who?
I walked Miles to get here! I'm glad you're home!

Knock Knock Jokes For Funny Kids

Knock knock.
Who's there?
Mint.
Mint who?
I mint to tell you - You're doorbell is broken!

Knock knock.
Who's there?
Theodore.
Theodore who?
Theodore seems to be really hard to open! Is it stuck?

Knock knock.
Who's there?
Wheel.
Wheel who?
Wheel be back in just a minute! Please wait here!

Knock knock.
Who's there?
Bud.
Bud who?
Bud I really want to know - where is the doorbell?

Jimmy Jones

Knock knock.
Who's there?
Goliath.
Goliath who?
Goliath down if you're a bit sleepy!

Knock knock.
Who's there?
Wendy.
Wendy who?
Wendy doorbell works, please let me know!

Knock knock.
Who's there?
Maya.
Maya who?
Maya come in? It's an emergency!

Knock knock.
Who's there?
Quack.
Quack who?
These jokes totally quack me up! Shall we read them all again?

Thank you so much

For reading our book.

I hope you have enjoyed these knock knock jokes as much as my kids and I did as we were putting this book together.

We really had a lot of fun and laughter creating and compiling this book and we really appreciate you for reading our book.

If you could possibly let us know what you thought of our book by way of a review we would really appreciate it 😊

To see all our latest books or leave a review just go to
kidsjokebooks.com
Once again, thanks so much for reading.

All the best,
Jimmy Jones
And also Ella & Alex (the kids)
And even Obi (the dog – he's very cute!)